T0132136

Annie's SHOES

R. BARDOEL

Balboa Press books may be ordered through booksellers or by contacting:

Balboa Press
A Division of Hay House
1663 Liberty Drive
Bloomington, IN 47403
www.balboapress.com
1 (877) 407-4847

ISBN: 978-1-9822-3940-4 (sc)
ISBN: 978-1-9822-3941-1 (e)

Library of Congress Control Number: 2019919756

Print information available on the last page.

Balboa Press rev. date: 01/06/2020

BALBOA.PRESS
A DIVISION OF HAY HOUSE

Annie's
SHOES

R. BARDOEL

"Hello", my name is Annie,
And these are my blue shoes.
They are the best shoes!

The very first day I got my blue shoes
I could ride my bicycle with no training wheels.

And the next day I won the race at the block party!

I also caught my first frog in these blue shoes.

And we even got our first family dog!
These are the best shoes ever!

I would like to keep my blue shoes forever!
They fit me just right.

Well, the truth is, if I step on the backs of them its better.
And there is an "almost" hole in the right shoe's toe.
Even so, they are the best!

When I sit beside Nancy at school, I hide
my right shoe behind my left.
Nancy dresses nice. Nancy also gets new shoes often!
She would see the "almost" hole in my shoe for sure!

I guess my Mom saw it too, because she
says I have to get new shoes.
I am not happy about that. In fact I am sad!
I love these shoes!

On our way to Mr Harper's shoe store, I remember
how Mr Harper helped me get my blue shoes
which were the last pair and were not my size.
Mr Harper said I would grow into them, and Mom
bought them for me even though they were too big.

When we walked into the store Mr Harper
said hi to my Mom right away.

Then he looked at me for a long time and said,
"Annie you have grown so much!"
Then he looked at my shoes and smiled big.

"I see you grew into your blue shoes.
And, I see you also grew right out of them too!"
We all laughed because my toe had come right through.
...the almost hole was a real hole!

Mr Harper and my mom are talking and
I am looking for new shoes.
There are no shoes like my favorite shoes.
I am sad.
I can't even find any blue shoes.
There are no shoes I like at all!

Today I am wearing jeans and my favorite shirt.
It is nearly the same color as my new shoes.

In class we are working in groups. I sit right next to Nancy.
I see Nancy look down at my shoes and she says:
"You look nice today Annie"
Nancy is always polite.
So I ask her: "Do you like my new shoes?"

Nancy smiled and said: "Oh yes, I wanted
those shoes in my collection."
I must have I looked at her oddly, "collection?" I thought.
"You can come and see it on Saturday."
she said with a smile.

Mom is driving me to Nancy's house for the afternoon.
I am not sure I want to stay that long.
I don't know Nancy very well.
Mom walks right with me to the door and says:
"Hello Claire", when Nancy's mom opened it.
I guess she knows Nancy's mother!
Nancy waves me in and I scoot around the adults.

In Nancy's room I feel my eyes open so wide.
Nancy has shoes around her whole room!
They start with smaller shoes and keep getting bigger.
She tells me a story about each pair.
Soon I know more about Nancy than I do about my cousin!
I like Nancy!

Today I woke up thinking of Nancy's shoes.
I wanted to draw pictures of them for Nancy.
So I took my markers out and drew quickly.
I drew every pair of shoes I could remember.

Later on, when I went to the park to play, I thought,
"If I put my shoes in my bag, and play in my bare feet,
my shoes will stay new like Nancy's shoes."

Then I saw myself with dirty feet trying
to sneak by Mom to wash them.
How silly! I laughed to myself. Shoes are for
keeping my feet clean and safe!"

I walked by the stream looking for frogs,
then I saw a heart shaped stone.
I have been looking for a heart stone for so long!
What a great day! I love these shoes!

"Time to leave for school." I hear Mom call
from the kitchen the next morning.
But I am not ready.
I am having a bad day!
My colored shoe pages are all over the floor.
I am about to burst into tears when
my Mom opens my door.

She looks at my face and then at the floor.
Then she picks up all my pages in one minute flat!
I'm not even going to be late for school!

At recess I showed Nancy the drawings I made for her,
Nancy is excited. She likes them!
Nancy asks, "Can I keep them?"

"I love my new red shoes!" thinks Annie.
Since I got these shoes, I found my heart rock,
and I have a new friend!

Hi, my name is
Annie, and these
are my red shoes.
They are the
best shoes!

Dedicated to
Annie, Katie and Pop.

Printed in the United States
By Bookmasters